First U.S. Edition

First published in France as FAUT PAS CONFONDRE by Éditions du Seuil

Library of Congress Cataloging-in-Publication Data

Tullet, Hervé
    [Faut pas confondre.  English]
    Night/Day : a book of eye-catching opposites / Hervé Tullet.
    —1st U.S. ed.
        p.     cm.
    Summary: Illustrations with die-cut holes introduce such opposites as hot and cold, inside and outside, and full and empty.
    ISBN 0-316-84244-3
    1. English language—Synonyms and antonyms—Juvenile literature.
    [1. English language—Synonyms and antonyms.  2. Toy and movable books.]
    I. Title.
PE1591.TB513  1999
428'.1—dc21                                                      98-35357

10 9 8 7 6 5 4 3 2

Cover display type and subtitle type hand-lettered by Lou M. Pollack

Printed in China

Hervé Tullet

# NIGHT

# DAY

## A Book of Eye-Catching Opposites

Little, Brown and Company
Boston   New York   London

circle

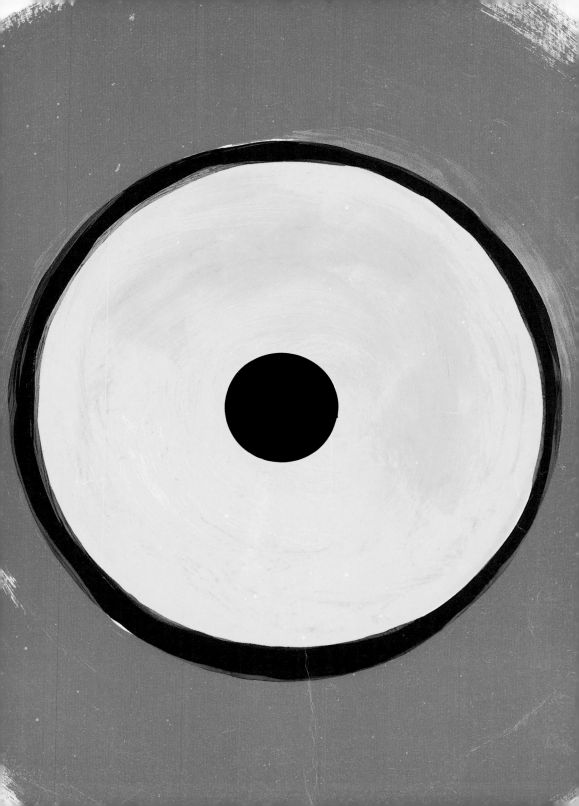

square

black and white

color

hot

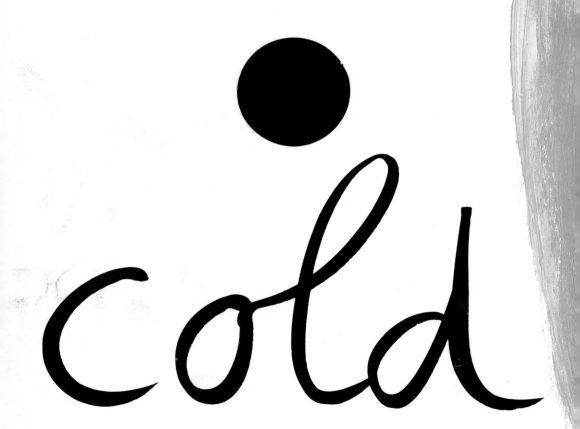

cold

little

big

boat

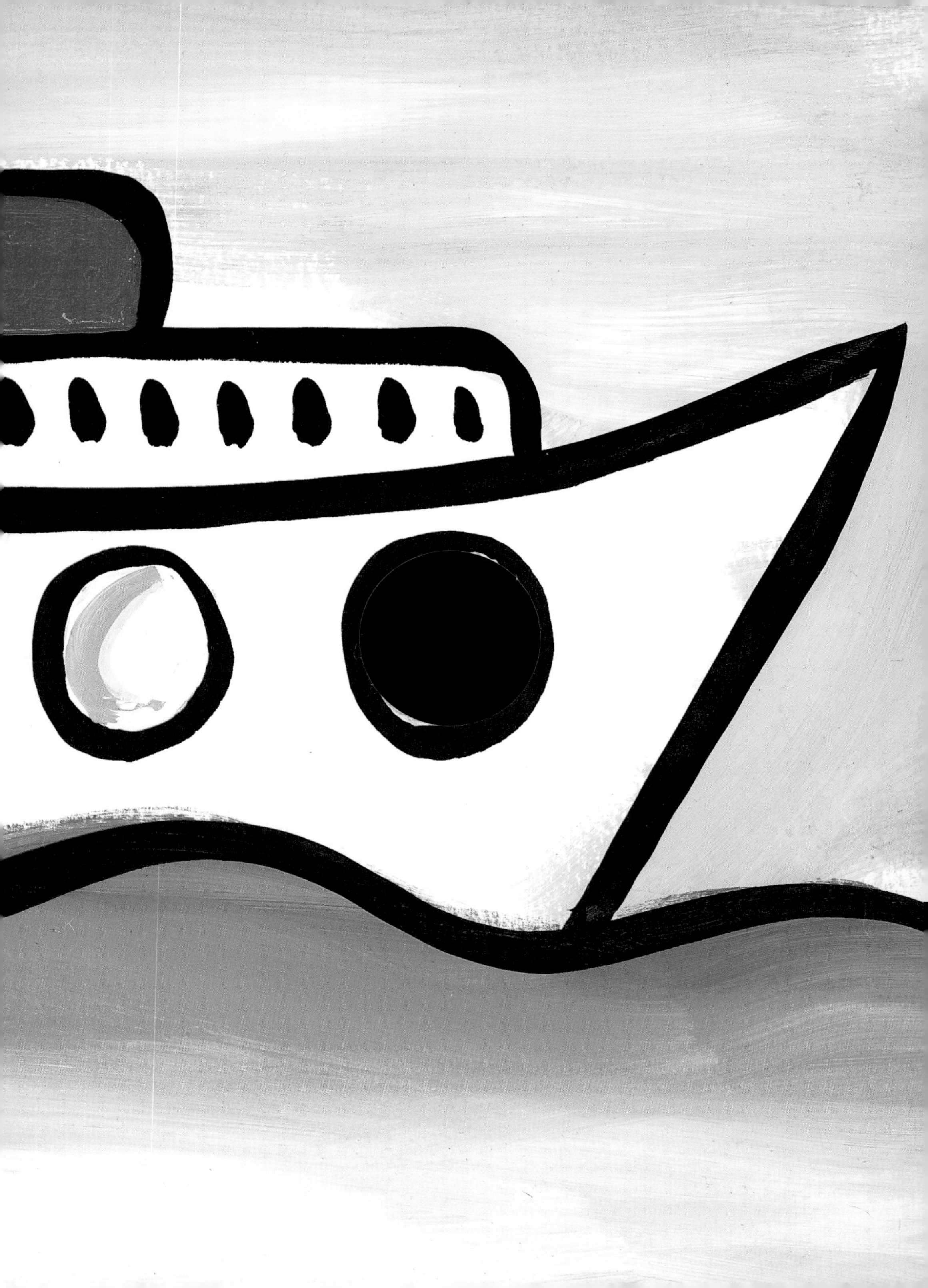

airplane

inside

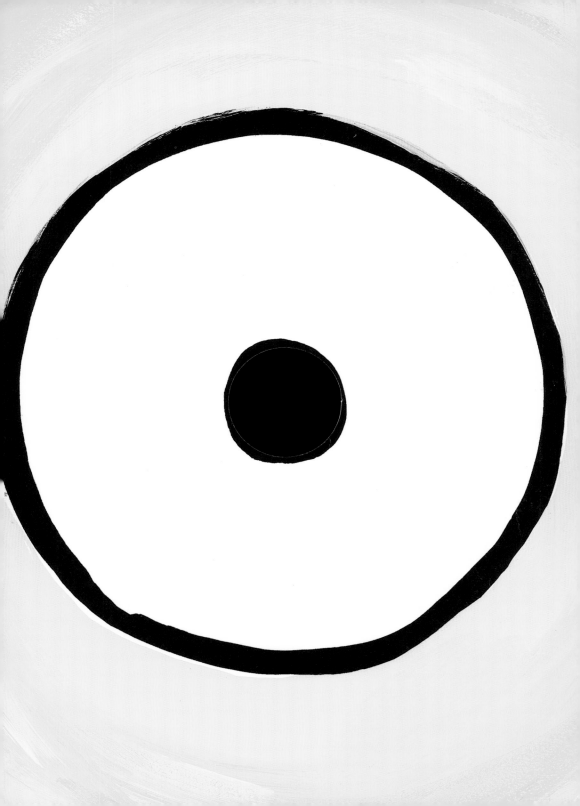

outside

foot

hand

*full*

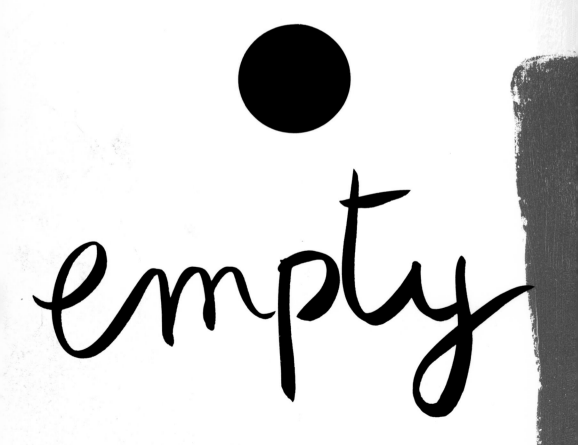

empty

intact

the same

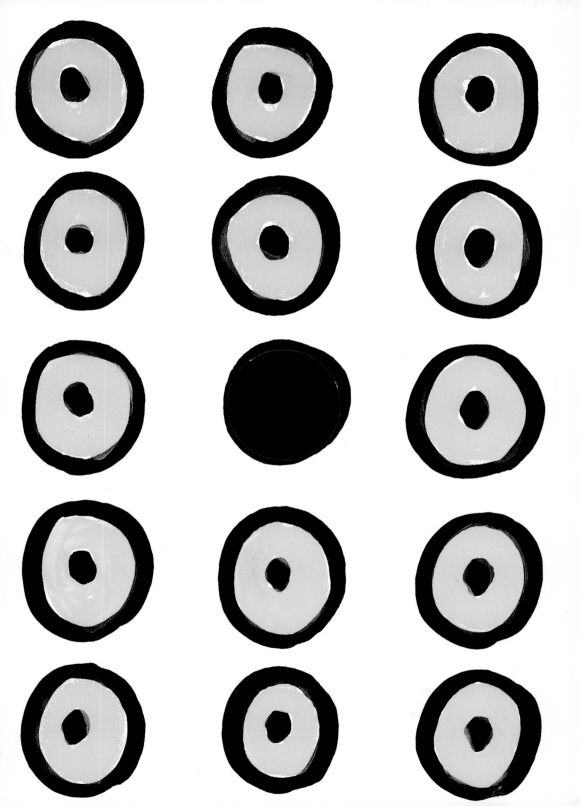

different

nice

naughty

Jan

near

up

down

light

clean

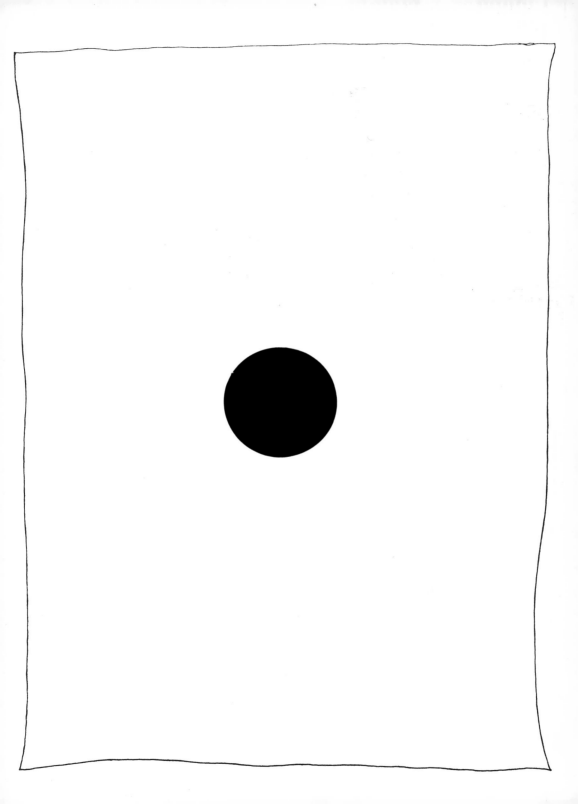

abstract

concrete li

light

shadow

order

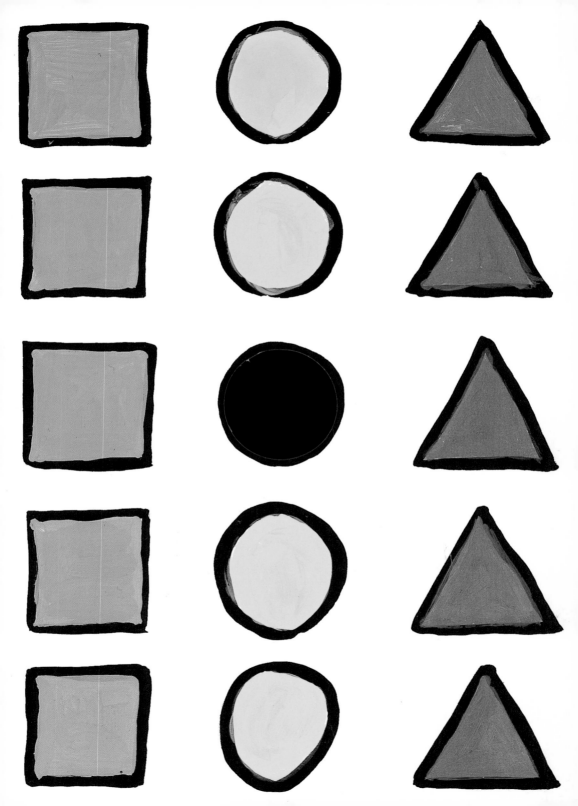

gentle

# pills

candy

above

underneath

everything

nothing

right

left

closed

open

together

apart

slow

fast

one

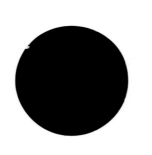

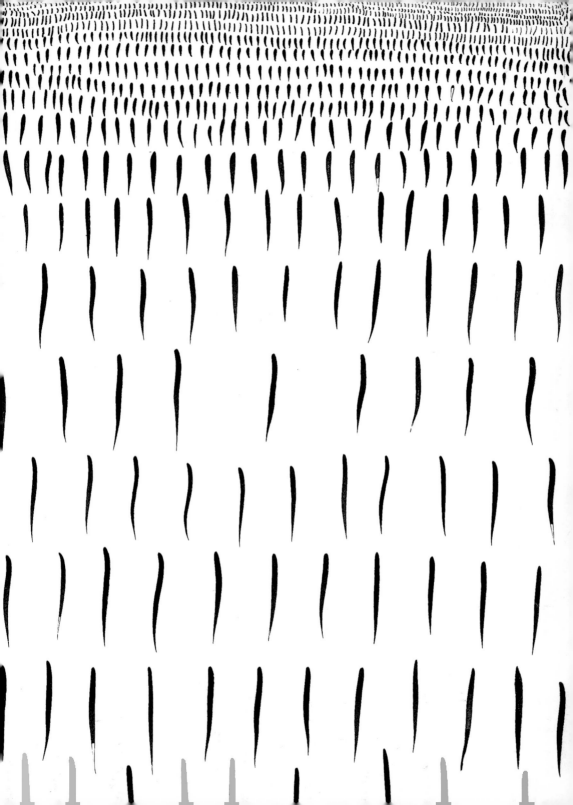

before

leaving

returning

vertical

ontal

ruined

grown-

baby

daddy